THE USBORNE
INTERNET-LINKED
FIRST
ATLAS

First published in 2003 by Usborne Publishing Ltd,
Usborne House, 83–85 Saffron Hill, London EC1N 8RT, England.

www.usborne.com

Printed in Portugal

Title page: A satellite image showing rivers joining the sea, along the coast of
Guinea-Bissau in west Africa. The red parts are land and the blue parts are water.
This page: These mountains and glaciers are on the island of Svalbard, which belongs
to Norway. The island is far inside the Arctic Circle and it's very cold there.

THE USBORNE
INTERNET-LINKED
FIRST ATLAS

Elizabeth Dalby

Designed by Laura Hammonds,
Candice Whatmore and Ruth Russell

Additional design: Adam Constantine, Michael Hill,
Karen Tomlins, Joanne Kirkby and Luke Sargent

Digital imagery by Keith Furnival

Edited by Kirsteen Rogers

Cover design: Zöe Wray

Cartography: European Map Graphics Ltd

Consultant: John Davidson

Consultant cartographic editor: Craig Asquith

Website adviser: Lisa Watts

Internet links

There are lots of exciting places on the Internet where you can find out more about the different countries, customs, people and animals in this book. The "Internet link" boxes in this book contain descriptions of websites you can visit by clicking on links on the Usborne Quicklinks Website.

Just go to **www.usborne-quicklinks.com** and enter the keywords "first atlas". Here are some of the things you can do on the websites described in this book:

- Find exciting games and activities from Africa

- Discover the creatures living on a coral reef

- Visit the Eiffel Tower

- Explore a virtual European castle

- Take an Arctic quiz

Safety on the Internet

Here are a few simple rules to help keep you safe while you are online:

- Ask your parent's or guardian's permission before you connect to the Internet.

- Never give out information such as your real name, address or telephone number.

- Never arrange to meet someone you started talking to on the Internet.

- If a site asks you to log in or register by typing your name or email address, ask permission from an adult first.

- If you receive an email from someone you don't know, tell an adult. Don't reply to it.

Site availability

The links in Usborne Quicklinks are regularly updated, but occasionally, you may get a message that a site is unavailable. This might be temporary, so try again later. If any of the sites close down, we will, if possible, replace them with alternatives. You will find an up-to-date list of sites at Usborne Quicklinks.

What you need

Most of the websites listed in this book can be accessed using a standard home computer and a web browser (the software that lets you look at information from the Internet). Some sites need extra programs (plug-ins) to play sound or show videos or animations. If you go to a site and do not have the necessary plug-in, a message will come up on the screen. There is usually a button on the site that you can click on to download the plug-in. Alternatively, go to **www.usborne-quicklinks.com** and click on Net Help. There, you can find links to download plug-ins.

Notes for parents

The websites described in this book are regularly reviewed and the links in Usborne Quicklinks are updated. However, the content of a website may change at any time and Usborne Publishing is not responsible for the content on any website other than its own. We recommend that children are supervised while on the Internet, that they do not use Internet Chat Rooms, and that you use Internet filtering software to block unsuitable material. Please ensure that your children read and follow the safety guidelines printed in the box on the left. For more information, see the Net Help area on the Usborne Quicklinks Website.

www.usborne-quicklinks.com

Go to **www.usborne-quicklinks.com** and enter the keywords "first atlas" for direct links to all the websites in this book.

Contents

These brightly painted houses are in Buenos Aires, the capital city of Argentina in South America.

About maps

An atlas is a collection of maps. Maps are pictures of areas, seen from above. They show places much smaller than they really are. Some maps show the whole world, and some show much smaller areas, like cities or streets.

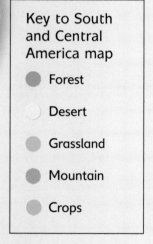

Rio Grande

Mississippi

Central America

Gulf of Mexico

Cuba

Caribbean Sea

Guiana Highlands

Amazon

Amazon Rainforest

SOUTH AMERICA

Andes

Atacama Desert

Pampas

Patagonia

Cape Horn

What will you see on a map?

Maps should be easy to understand. Different kinds of shading and symbols help show what a place is like. A key explains what they all mean.

The size of a map compared with the real-life area it shows is called its scale. Some maps have a line called a scale bar that shows you the real distances between places on the map.

Key to South and Central America map

● Forest
○ Desert
● Grassland
● Mountain
● Crops

This map shows what the land in South and Central America is like.

Scale

Scale bar ——
0km   2,000km
0 miles   1,240 miles

Which way is up?

The Earth doesn't really have a top and a bottom. Maps are often drawn with north at the top, though, to make them easier for everyone to understand.

This compass symbol shows which way is north (N), south (S), east (E) and west (W).

Sea and land

More than two-thirds of the Earth is covered in salty water – the seas and oceans. Maps usually show water in blue.

The rest of the Earth is covered in land. Maps sometimes shade the land as it would look from above. Grasslands are often green and deserts can be sandy brown or yellow.

An island is land with water all around it. This is one of the Solomon Islands, in the Pacific Ocean.

Countries and continents

The land is divided into seven huge areas called continents, which are split into smaller areas called countries. Each country is run by a government and has its own laws. Some large countries are further divided into states, to make them easier to run.

Internet link

For a link to a website where you can play a memory game about continents, go to **www.usborne-quicklinks.com**

This is the continent of North America. It is a large area of land and islands.

North America is divided into countries, including Canada, the USA and Mexico.

The USA is divided into 50 different states. Each state can make its own laws.

Information from maps

Maps can show different things about the same area. Some maps show where countries and cities are. Some show what the land looks like or what kinds of plants grow there.

Political maps show countries and place names. The lines between countries are called borders or boundaries.

Physical maps show what the land looks like. They show features like mountains, lakes and rivers.

Thematic maps show other information, such as what the land is used for, or how many people live there.

Weather and wildlife

Different parts of the world have their own weather patterns, plants and wildlife. These areas are called biomes. Deserts, grasslands and rainforests are biomes. They can all be shown on a thematic map.

These cacti live in the desert, where it hardly ever rains. They store water in their stems.

Internet link
For links to a website where you can find out more about biomes, go to **www.usborne-quicklinks.com**

How many people?

The people who live in an area are its population. Maps can be used to show which parts of an area are crowded, and which parts have very few people living in them.

This map of North America shows the areas where most people live.

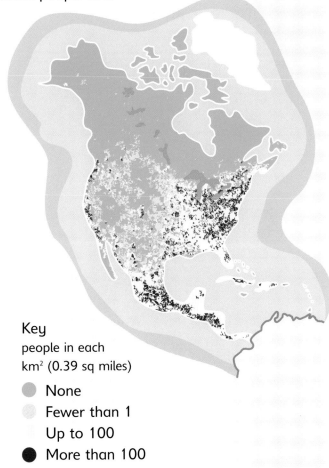

Key
people in each
km² (0.39 sq miles)

- None
- Fewer than 1
- Up to 100
- More than 100

Towns and cities

Anywhere where a group of people live is called a settlement. A village is a small settlement, a town is bigger, and the largest kind is a city. The capital city of a country is where its government is based. About half the people in the world live in a town or a city.

Lines on maps

To make it easy to measure distances and find places on a map, the Earth is divided up with imaginary lines. The two sets of lines are called longitude and latitude. They are numbered in degrees (°) and minutes (′).

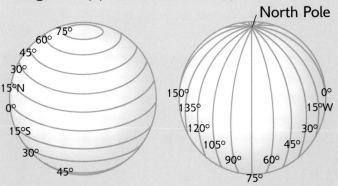

Lines of latitude run around the globe. On maps they usually run from left to right.

Longitude lines run from the North to the South Pole, and usually from top to bottom on maps.

This drawing of the Earth shows the North Pole and the main lines of longitude and latitude.

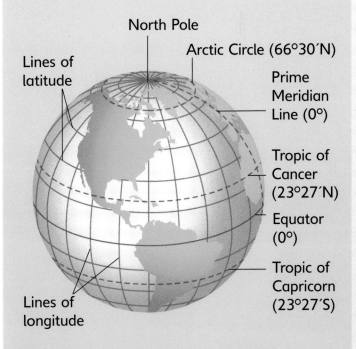

This globe is tipped slightly forward so the North Pole shows. This means that you can't quite see the South Pole.

The world's land

This is a physical map. It shows the different kinds of land in each continent.

The top half of the globe is called the northern hemisphere.

The bottom half of the globe is called the southern hemisphere.

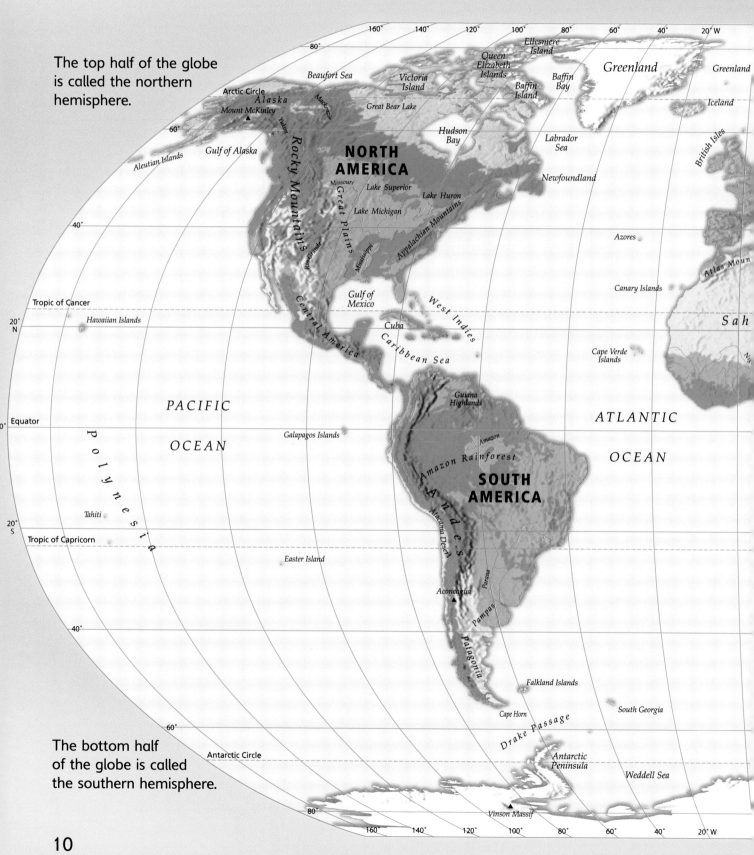

80°

160° 140° 120° 100° 80° 60° 40° 20° W

Ellesmere Island
Queen Elizabeth Islands
Baffin Bay
Baffin Island
Greenland
Greenland
Iceland
British Isles

Beaufort Sea
Victoria Island
Great Bear Lake
Hudson Bay
Labrador Sea

Arctic Circle
Alaska
Mount McKinley
Mackenzie
Yukon

60°

Aleutian Islands
Gulf of Alaska
Rocky Mountains
Missouri
Great Plains
Lake Superior
Lake Huron
Lake Michigan
Mississippi
Appalachian Mountains
Newfoundland

NORTH AMERICA

40°

Rio Grande
Azores
Atlas Moun

Tropic of Cancer
20° N
Hawaiian Islands
Gulf of Mexico
Central America
Cuba
West Indies
Caribbean Sea
Canary Islands
S a h
Cape Verde Islands
Nig

PACIFIC
OCEAN
Polynesia

Galapagos Islands
Guiana Highlands
Amazon
Amazon Rainforest
ATLANTIC
OCEAN

Equator
0°

Tahiti
Andes
Atacama Desert
SOUTH AMERICA

20° S
Tropic of Capricorn
Easter Island
Aconcagua
Paraná
Pampas

40°
Patagonia
Falkland Islands

Cape Horn
South Georgia
Drake Passage

60°
Antarctic Circle
Antarctic Peninsula
Weddell Sea

80°
Vinson Massif

160° 140° 120° 100° 80° 60° 40° 20° W

10

Key to map of the world's land

- ● Forest
- ● Grassland
- ○ Desert
- ● Mountain (only high mountains are shown)
- ○ Tundra areas (frozen ground with no trees)
- ○ Ice (areas where the ice or snow never melts)
- ● Crops (land used for growing plants for people and animals to eat)
- ○ Sea
- ● Lake or inland sea
- — River
- ▲ Mountain peak

Scale

0km — 3,000km
0 miles — 1,860 miles

ARCTIC OCEAN

40° 60° 80° 100° 120° 140° 160° 180° 80°

valbard
North Cape
Novaya Zemlya
Kara Sea
Severnaya Zemlya
Laptev Sea
New Siberia Islands
East Siberian Sea
Barents Sea
navia

Ural Mountains
Ob
Yenisey
Siberia
Verkhoyansk Range
Lena
Arctic Circle
Bering Sea
60°

ROPE

Danube
Volga
Mount Elbrus ▲
Black Sea
Caspian Sea
Aral Sea
Altai Mountains
Lake Baikal
Amur
Sea of Okhotsk
Kamchatka Peninsula

terranean Sea
ASIA
Gobi Desert
Sea of Japan
Japan
40°

Libyan Desert
Nile
Arabia
Red Sea
Himalayas
Indus
Ganges
Mount Everest
Yangtze
China
Yellow
Honshu

Rub al Khali (Empty Quarter)
Mount Everest
East China Sea
PACIFIC
Tropic of Cancer

ert
India
Arabian Sea
Bay of Bengal
Mekong
Taiwan
20° N

FRICA
Ethiopian Highlands
Luzon
Philippines
Micronesia
OCEAN

e l
Cape Comorin
Sri Lanka
South China Sea
Mindanao

Lake Victoria
Seychelles
Sumatra
Borneo
Celebes
New Guinea
Equator 0°

Kilimanjaro ▲
INDIAN
Java Sea
Mount Wilhelm ▲
Solomon Islands
Melanesia

Comoro Islands
OCEAN
Java
Arafura Sea

Zambezi
Madagascar
Coral Sea
Fiji Islands

Mauritius
Great Barrier Reef
New Caledonia
20° S
Tropic of Capricorn

Great Sandy Desert
O C E A N I A

Great Victoria Desert
Great Dividing Range

Tasman Sea
North Island

a Hope
Kerguelen Islands
Tasmania
South Island
40°

60°

SOUTHERN OCEAN
Antarctic Circle

A N T A R C T I C A

40° 60° 80° 100° 120° 140° 160° 180°

Ross Sea
80°

Countries of the world

This is a political map. It shows the different countries that make up each continent. Can you find your country on the map?

Key to map of countries of the world

— Border, where one country is joined to the next one

— Coast

⬤ Lake or inland sea

Some country names had to be shortened to fit on the map. This list has the names written in full.
ARM. Armenia
AUST. Austria
AZER. Azerbaijan
BELG. Belgium

B.H. Boznia and Herzegovina
CRO. Croatia
CZECH REP. Czech Republic
LEB. Lebanon
LUX. Luxembourg
MAC. Macedonia

NETH. Netherlands
SLOV. Slovenia
S.M. Serbia and Montenegro
SWITZ. Switzerland
U.A.E United Arab Emirates

Scale

0km — 3,000km
0 miles — 1,860 miles

ARCTIC OCEAN

Arctic Circle

RUSSIA

FINLAND
ESTONIA
LATVIA
LITHUANIA
...AND
BELARUS
UKRAINE
...EP
...OVAKIA
MOLDOVA
...NGARY
ROMANIA
Black Sea
...S.M.
BULGARIA
...MAC
GREECE
TURKEY
CYPRUS LEB.
SYRIA
ISRAEL
JORDAN
IRAQ
KUWAIT
BAHRAIN
QATAR
U.A.E.
OMAN
...ranean Sea
...BYA
EGYPT
SAUDI ARABIA
YEMEN
...HAD
SUDAN
ERITREA
DJIBOUTI
ETHIOPIA
SOMALIA
...CENTRAL AFRICAN REPUBLIC
UGANDA
KENYA
CONGO (DEMOCRATIC REPUBLIC)
RWANDA
BURUNDI
TANZANIA
...OLA
ZAMBIA
MALAWI
COMOROS
...A
ZIMBABWE
MADAGASCAR
MAURITIUS
BOTSWANA
MOZAMBIQUE
Reunion (France)
SWAZILAND
SOUTH AFRICA
LESOTHO

KAZAKHSTAN
GEORGIA
ARM. AZER.
Caspian Sea
UZBEKISTAN
KYRGYZSTAN
TURKMENISTAN
TAJIKISTAN
IRAN
AFGHANISTAN
PAKISTAN
NEPAL
BHUTAN
INDIA
BANGLA DESH
BURMA (MYANMAR)
LAOS
THAILAND
CAMBODIA
VIETNAM
SRI LANKA
MALDIVES
SEYCHELLES

MONGOLIA

CHINA

NORTH KOREA
SOUTH KOREA
JAPAN

TAIWAN

PHILIPPINES

PACIFIC OCEAN

Tropic of Cancer

Northern Mariana Islands (U.S.A.)

PALAU

FEDERATED STATES OF MICRONESIA

MARSHALL ISLANDS

20° N

MALAYSIA
SINGAPORE
BRUNEI

INDONESIA

EAST TIMOR

PAPUA NEW GUINEA

SOLOMON ISLANDS

NAURU

KIRIBATI

TUVALU

Equator 0°

Coral Sea Islands Territory (Australia)

VANUATU

New Caledonia (France)

SAMOA

FIJI TONGA

20° S

INDIAN OCEAN

AUSTRALIA

Tropic of Capricorn

Kerguelen Islands (France)

40°

NEW ZEALAND

...EAN

60°

Antarctic Circle

ANTARCTICA

80°

40° 60° 80° 100° 120° 140° 160° 180°

North America

This continent includes three huge countries – Canada, the USA and Mexico. It also includes the Caribbean islands and the countries in the strip of land that joins onto South America.

Key to North America map

- ■ Capital city
- ○ Major city or town
- ▬ Border (where one country joins another one)
- ── River
- ▬ Coast

Scale

0km	1,000km
0 miles	620 miles

Raccoons live in North and Central America. They usually sleep in trees during the day and come out at night to feed.

Internet link

For a link to a website with lots of North and Central America maps to print, label and shade in, go to **www.usborne-quicklinks.com**

Hawaiian Islands (U.S.A.)

Arctic Circle

ARCTIC OCEAN

Queen Elizabeth Islands

Bering Strait

Point Barrow

Beaufort Sea

Parry Isla

Bering Sea

Yukon

ALASKA (U.S.A.)

Victoria Island

Mount McKinley ▲

○ Anchorage

Mackenzie

Great Bear Lake

Gulf of Alaska

R O C K Y   M O U N T A I N S

Great Slave Lake

C A N A

Lake Athabas

Reindeer Lake

○ Calgary

Vancouver ■

G r e a t

Winr

○ Seattle

Columbia

PACIFIC OCEAN

Great Plains

Mi

Great Salt Lake

San Francisco ○

California

U N I T E D   S T A T E

(U

Colorado

Denver ○

Los Angeles ○

○ Phoenix

Lower California

Ciudad Juarez ○

Te x

Rio G

○ Hermosillo

Tropic of Cancer

Monterrey

MEXICO

○ Guadala

Mexico Cit

Acapulco ○

14

GREENLAND
(Denmark)

Greenland is part of North America, but it belongs to Denmark, in Europe.

Baffin Bay

Baffin Island

Godthab

Cape Farewell

Labrador Sea

Hudson Bay

Labrador Peninsula

Newfoundland

St. John's

nnipeg

Quebec

St. Lawrence

Quebec

Nova Scotia

Halifax

Lake Superior

Montreal

Ottawa

Lake Huron

Boston

nneapolis

Toronto

Lake Ontario

ake Michigan

Detroit

Lake Erie

New York

Chicago

Pittsburgh

Philadelphia

A M E R I C A

St. Louis

Cincinnati

Washington, D.C.

City

Ohio

Arkansas

Mississippi

Appalachian Mountains

Cape Hatteras

Atlanta

Florida

ATLANTIC OCEAN

uston

New Orleans

Gulf of Mexico

Miami

THE BAHAMAS

Nassau

This photograph was taken from space by a satellite. The orange parts are deserts. The brown areas are the Rocky Mountains.

Tropic of Cancer

Havana

Puerto Rico (U.S.A.)

ST. KITTS AND NEVIS

CUBA

DOMINICAN REPUBLIC

HAITI

ANTIGUA AND BARBUDA

Guadeloupe (France)

Merida

Port-au-Prince

Santo Domingo

DOMINICA

Martinique (France)

acruz

Yucatan Peninsula

ST. LUCIA

BARBADOS

JAMAICA

Kingston

ST. VINCENT AND THE GRENADINES

Caribbean Sea

GRENADA

BELIZE

Belmopan

TRINIDAD AND TOBAGO

GUATEMALA

HONDURAS

Port-of-Spain

emala City

Tegucigalpa

San Salvador

EL SALVADOR

NICARAGUA

Managua

San Jose

Panama City

COSTA RICA

PANAMA

North America facts

Total land area 22,656,190km² *(8,745,289 sq miles)*

Biggest country Canada 9,970,610km² *(3,849,653 sq miles)*

Smallest country St. Kitts and Nevis 269km² *(104 sq miles)*

Biggest island Greenland 2,175,600km² *(840,000 sq miles)*

Highest mountain Mount McKinley, Alaska, USA 6,194m *(20,321ft)*

Longest river Mississippi/ Missouri, USA 6,019km *(3,741 miles)*

Biggest lake Lake Superior, USA/Canada 82,414km² *(31,820 sq miles)*

Highest waterfall Yosemite Falls, California, USA 739m *(2,425ft)*

Biggest desert Great Basin Desert, USA 492,000km² *(190,000 sq miles)*

Using the land

Much of the land in North America is hard to live and work on. Some areas are hot and rocky, and some are freezing and snowy. In other parts of North America, the land and weather are just right for farming.

Shapes in the rock

In the southwest USA, some of the rocky land has slowly been worn away by rivers to make channels called canyons. Strong winds and rain have worn the rock away even more, making strange, rippling shapes.

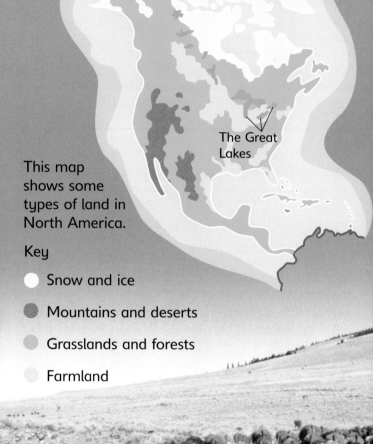

This map shows some types of land in North America.

The Great Lakes

Key

● Snow and ice

● Mountains and deserts

● Grasslands and forests

● Farmland

This strange photograph shows part of a small canyon in Arizona. The orange rock is called sandstone and the big cat is a puma.

Shaking ground

The Earth's crust is made up of huge slabs of rock, called plates. Sometimes they push or slide against each other, making the ground shake. This is called an earthquake. The San Andreas Fault, in the west of the USA, is a place where two plates slide past each other. Earthquakes often happen there.

This house fell down after a big earthquake in San Francisco, a city on the San Andreas Fault.

Massive farms

In the USA, Canada and Mexico, there are many huge cattle farms, called ranches. The cattle are farmed for their meat and skins. Other farms in North America grow crops such as corn and vegetables in enormous fields.

Internet link

For a link to a website with a clickable map and photographs of the biggest canyon in the world, go to **www.usborne-quicklinks.com**

One of the best ways for cowboys to move around their land and round up cattle is on horseback. Some farms are so big it would take days to walk across them.

17

Cities and celebrations

Explorers from Europe arrived in North America a few hundred years ago. But people have lived there for many thousands of years. Today, people come from all over the world to live there.

This map shows where some early North American people lived.

Key

- Aztecs
- Maya
- Native American tribes

Inuit
Inuit
Chipewyan
Cree
Inuit
Cree
Blackfoot
Chippewa
Chinook
Crow
Cheyenne
Huron
Cherokee
Comanche
Sioux
Iroquois
Hopi
Chickshaw
Creek
Navajo
Chocktaw
Apache
Yucatan Peninsula

Stone cities

The Maya and the Aztec people lived in Mexico before European settlers came. The Maya built beautiful cities and pyramid-shaped temples out of stone. Ruins of these can still be seen today, on the Yucatan Peninsula in Mexico.

This Mayan temple is over 1,000 years old.

The Maya believed their kings were gods and built temples like this one to worship them.

Busy city

New York City is the biggest city in the USA, and also one of the largest cities in the world. Almost 20 million people live there, and thousands more visit every year.

Internet link

For a link to a website where you can find lots more information about New York and see a slide show, go to **www.usborne-quicklinks.com**

Part of New York is on an island called Manhattan. Bridges join Manhattan to the rest of the city.

Icy homeland

Inuit people live in the icy north of Canada, in an area called Nunavut. It's too cold to grow crops there, so Inuit hunters catch animals and fish for people to eat.

This Inuit man is making a harpoon spear to take hunting. He is wearing warm fur clothes.

Calypso music

People visit the Caribbean islands for warm weather and sandy beaches. The islands are also famous for calypso music, which people play on drums made out of old oil cans.

This girl is dressed for Trinidad's carnival. Dancing and music are an important part of the celebrations.

South America

South America stretches down from the equator almost as far as the Antarctic. It is joined to North America by a narrow strip of land at the edge of Colombia.

Key to South America map

- ■ Capital city
- ○ Major city or town
- ── Border (where one country joins another one)
- ── River
- ▬ Coast

Scale

0km	1,000km
0 miles	620 miles

This is a toucan. Toucans live in South American rainforests. They use their long beaks to pick and eat fruit from the trees.

Caribbean Sea

Maracaibo ■ Caracas

VENEZUELA

Medellin

■ **Bogota**

Guiana Highl

Cali **COLOMBIA** *Orinoco*

Equator

Galapagos Islands (Ecuador)

□ **Quito**

ECUADOR

Guayaquil

Negro

Amazon

Amazon Rainfore

PERU

Ucayali

A N D E S

Lima ■

Lake Titicaca **BOLIVIA**

■ **La Paz**

Atacama Desert

■ **Sucre**

Tropic of Capricorn

PACIFIC

OCEAN

CHILE

San Mig de Tucu

A N D E S

Cordoba ○

Aconcagua ▲ Ros

Santiago ■

ARGENTI

Pam

Patagonia

Strait of Magell

Tierra del Fue

Cape Horn

Drake Pass

ATLANTIC

OCEAN

orgetown
Paramaribo
NA   Cayenne
RINAM   FRENCH
         GUIANA
         (France)

Equator

Reservoir   Amazon   Belem

Xingu   Tucurui Reservoir   Fortaleza

s

B R A Z I L   Tocantins   Sobradinho   Recife
                          Reservoir

Plateau of   São Francisco   Brazilian Highlands   Salvador
Mato Grosso

Goiania   Brasilia

Belo Horizonte

Parana   Furnas
         Reservoir   Rio de Janeiro

AGUAY   São Paulo

Asuncion   Tropic of Capricorn

Curitiba

Porto Alegre

ATLANTIC

OCEAN

URUGUAY

Montevideo

enos Aires

and Islands
(U.K.)

Internet link

For a link to a website with South
America maps to print, label and shade in,
go to **www.usborne-quicklinks.com**

This is what South America looks
like from space. The mottled strip
along the west coast shows the
Andes Mountains.

South America facts

Total land area *17,866,130km²
(6,898,113 sq miles)*

Biggest country Brazil *8,547,400km²
(3,300,151 sq miles)*

Smallest country Surinam *163,270km²
(63,039 sq miles)*

Biggest island Tierra del Fuego *46,360km²
(17,900 sq miles)*

Highest mountain Aconcagua, Argentina
6,959m (22,831ft)

Longest river Amazon, Brazil *6,440km
(4,000 miles)*

Biggest lake Lake Maracaibo, Venezuela
13,312km² (5,140 sq miles)

Highest waterfall Angel Falls,
on the Churun River, Venezuela
979m (3,212ft)

Biggest desert Patagonian Desert,
Argentina *673,000km²
(260,000 sq miles)*

Wettest and driest

South America has one of the wettest places on Earth in it – the Amazon Rainforest. But it also has the Atacama Desert, which is one of the driest. South America's Andes Mountains make up the the longest chain of mountains in the world.

Snowy peaks

The Andes Mountains are over 7,000km (4,300 miles) long, and stretch all the way down the continent. The lower slopes are good for farming, but the high peaks are snowy and bleak. More than 30 of the peaks in the Andes are volcanoes.

This map shows some of the landscape features of South America.

This climber is close to the top of Huascaran, one of the highest peaks in the Andes.

Key

Amazon Rainforest

Rivers in the Amazon

Atacama Desert

Andes Mountains

Forest homes

The Amazon Rainforest is the biggest rainforest in the world. It's always hot there and it rains nearly every day. The forest is home to a huge number of plants and animals.

This blue morpho butterfly comes from the Amazon. It's as big as a man's hand.

Internet link

For a link to a website where you can take a walk through a rainforest, meeting animals along the way, go to **www.usborne-quicklinks.com**

Dry ground

The Atacama Desert, in Chile, is next to the Pacific Ocean but it is the driest place on the planet. In some parts of the desert, people think it may never have rained at all.

Desert plants like these have long roots to reach way down into the cracked earth for water.

Mighty river

There's more water in the Amazon River than in any other river in the world. Over 1,000 smaller rivers flow into it, from all over the north part of South America. It is also one of the longest rivers, and winds nearly all the way across the top of the continent.

This boy is paddling his boat along the Amazon River. The main part of the river is so wide there are no bridges over it.

23

Places for living

South Americans live high in the mountains, deep in the rainforest, and even in the desert. Many people live in tiny farming villages, but South America also has some of the biggest cities in the world.

This map shows the places where most people live in South America.

Key
people in each km²
(0.39 sq miles)

- None
- Fewer than 1
- Up to 100
- More than 100

The Uros people use boats made of reeds to cross Lake Titicaca.

Mountain lake

Lake Titicaca is high up in the Andes Mountains, near Peru and Bolivia. The Uros people live by the lake and go fishing in its icy waters. Some of them live on floating islands made of reeds.

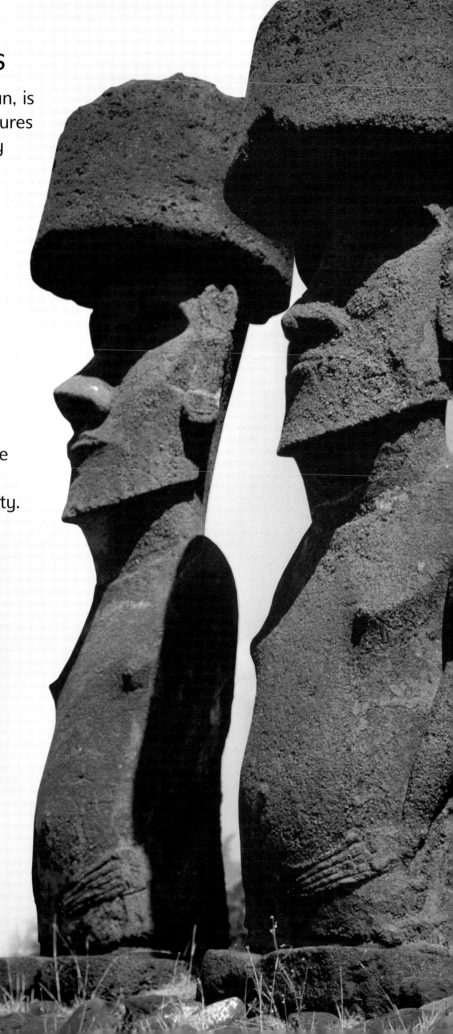

Mysterious statues

Easter Island, in the Pacific Ocean, is covered in hundreds of stone figures called *moai*. They were made by the first people who lived there, to worship their ancestors.

Most *moai* statues are at least twice the height of a man, and very heavy. How they were moved into place is a mystery.

City celebration

Early every year, the busy city of Rio de Janeiro in Brazil holds a carnival. It lasts for five days, with feasting, music and costume parades. Dancers take part in samba competitions across the city.

At carnival time in Rio de Janeiro, floats like this one carry costumed people through the streets of the city.

Internet link

For a link to a website with pictures of Andean people and songs to listen to, go to **www.usborne-quicklinks.com**

Asia

Asia is the biggest continent. It stretches from the Arctic Circle to the equator, and from the Ural Mountains in the west to the Pacific Ocean in the east.

The part of Russia on this side of the Ural Mountains is in Europe.

Key to Asia map

- ■ Capital city
- ○ Major city or town
- ▬ Border (where one country joins another one)
- River
- Coast

Scale

0km   1,000km
0 miles   640 miles

ARCTIC OCEAN

Novaya Zemlya
Barents Sea
Kara Sea
Arctic Circle

St. Petersburg
Arkhangelsk
No

Moscow
Nizhniy Novgorod
Kazan
Yekaterinburg
Ural Mountains
Ob
Yenisey
R U S

Volga
Samara
Chelyabinsk
Irtysh
Ob
Omsk
Novosibirsk

Istanbul
Black Sea
Rostov
Astrakhan
Aqtobe
Astana
Altai Mou

Mediterranean Sea
Izmir
Ankara
Caspian Sea
KAZAKHSTAN
Lake Balkhash

TURKEY
GEORGIA
Caucasus
Aral Sea
Almaty
Urumq

Nicosia
Tbilisi
ARMENIA **Yerevan**
AZERBAIJAN
UZBEKISTAN

CYPRUS
Beirut
SYRIA
Baku
Bishkek

LEBANON **Damascus**
Tabriz
TURKMENISTAN
Tashkent **KYRGYZSTAN**

ISRAEL
Euphrates
Tigris
Ashgabat
Dushanbe

Jerusalem
Amman
Baghdad
Kunlun Mount

JORDAN
Tehran
TAJIKISTAN

Syrian Desert
IRAQ
Mashhad
Plateau of Tibet

Basra
IRAN
AFGHANISTAN
HIMALAYAS

Medina
KUWAIT
Kabul
Islamabad
Lh

SAUDI
Shiraz
Kandahar
Delhi

ARABIA
BAHRAIN
PAKISTAN
NEPAL

Jedda
QATAR
Indus
New Delhi
Mount Ever

Mecca
Riyadh
Abu Dhabi
Thar Desert
Kathmandu

UNITED ARAB
Muscat
Ganges
BHU

EMIRATES
Karachi
Varanasi
BANGLADESH

Rub al Khali
(Empty Quarter)
OMAN
Nagpur
Dhaka

Sana
Kolkata
(Calcutta)

YEMEN
Arabian Sea
Mumbai
(Bombay)
INDIA
Bay
Ben

Aden
Socotra
(Yemen)

Giant pandas live in bamboo forests in the high mountains of west China. These days, there are fewer than 1,000 giant pandas left in the wild.

Bangalore
Chennai
(Madras)

Cape Comorin
SRI LANKA

Colombo
Sri Jayewardenepura Kotte

MALDIVES
Male
Equator

Internet link

For a link to a website with lots of maps of Asia to print out, label and shade in, go to **www.usborne-quicklinks.com**

INDIAN OCEAN

East
Siberian
Sea

Anadyr

Bering Sea

*Laptev
Sea*

Arctic Circle

Verkhoyansk Range

Lena

Okhotsk

*Kamchatka
Peninsula*

Petropavlovsk-
Kamchatskiy

Yakutsk

*Sea of
Okhotsk*

eria

Lena

Komsomolsk

Amur

Hokkaido

Sapporo

kutsk

Lake Baikal

Qiqihar

*Sea of
Japan*

JAPAN

Ulan Bator

MONGOLIA

Shenyang

**NORTH
KOREA**
Pyongyang

Tokyo

Honshu

Osaka

Beijing

Seoul

Hiroshima

bi Desert

Baotou

**SOUTH
KOREA**

Yellow

*East China
Sea*

C H I N A

Xian

Shanghai
Hangzhou

Tropic of Cancer

Chongqing

Yangtze

Fuzhou

Taipei

TAIWAN

P A C I F I C

Kunming

Xianggang (Hong Kong)

O C E A N

MA
MAR

Hanoi

Hainan

Luzon

LAOS
Vientiane

*South China
Sea*

PHILIPPINES

angoon

Mekong

Manila

Philippine Sea

THAILAND

VIETNAM

angkok

CAMBODIA

Mindanao

**Phnom
Penh**

Ho Chi Minh City
(Saigon)

Davao

Equator

BRUNEI

MALAYSIA

New Guinea

Kuala Lumpur

SINGAPORE

Borneo

Celebes

Banda Sea

dan

I N D O N E S I A

Palembang

Java Sea

Ujung Pandang

Arafura Sea

Sumatra

Jakarta
Surabaya

Dili
EAST TIMOR

Java

Timor Sea

The white ridges across
the middle of this satellite
photograph of Asia are
the snowy mountaintops
of the Himalayas.

Asia facts

Total land area
*44,537,920km²
(17,196,090 sq miles)*

Biggest country Russia
*Total area: 17,075,200km²
(6,592,735 sq miles) Asiatic Russia:
12,780,800km² (4,934,667 sq miles)*

Smallest country Maldives
300km² (116 sq miles)

Biggest island Borneo
751,100km² (290,000 sq miles)

Highest mountain Mount
Everest, Nepal/China *8,850m
(29,035ft)*

Longest river Yangtze
*(Chang Jiang), China 6,380km
(3,964 miles)*

Biggest lake Caspian Sea,
western Asia *370,999km²
(143,243 sq miles)*

Highest waterfall Jog Falls, India
253m (830ft)

Biggest desert Arabian Desert
*(deserts of Saudi Arabia)
2,230,000km² (900,000 sq miles)*

27

All kinds of land

Asia has almost every kind of landscape you can think of. In the north, there are freezing forests. To the south, there are deserts and rainforests. Much of central Asia is covered in grassland.

Rice terraces

Some parts of Asia are very hilly. Farmers there make flat shelves called terraces in the land, to grow their crops on. The terraces stop water from running away down the slope, so the rice can grow. Many Asian farmers grow rice in this way.

These hillside terraces make flat areas for rice crops to grow.

High mountains

The highest mountains in the world are the Himalayas. They run through India, Nepal, Bhutan and China. The tallest peak is Mount Everest. Each year, many climbers try to reach the top.

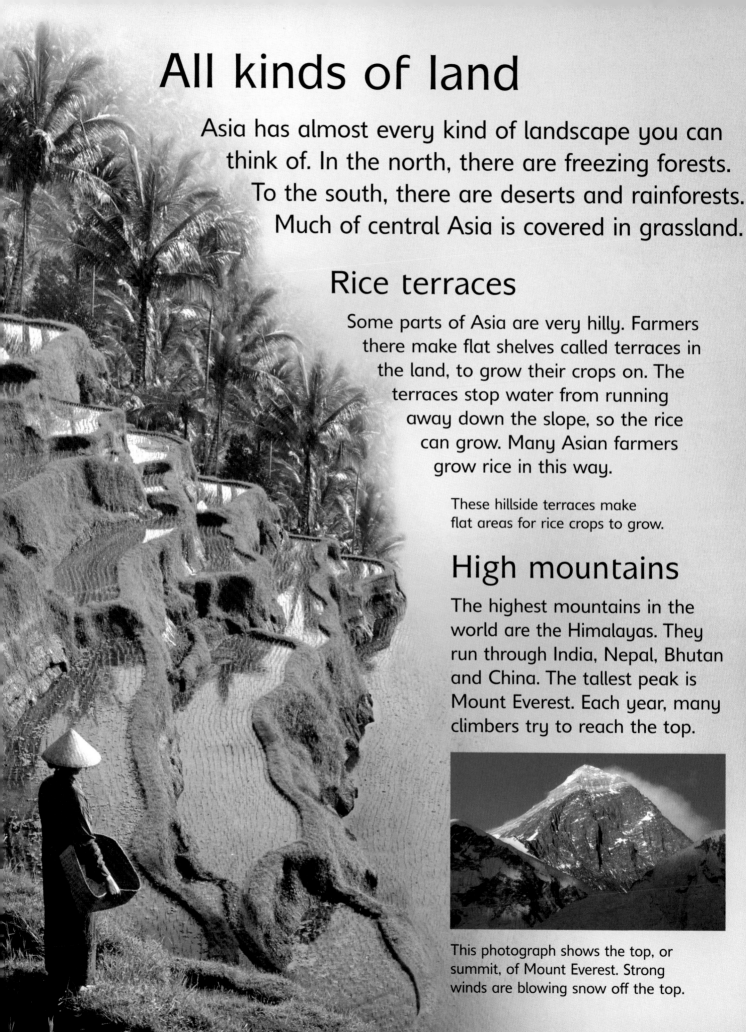

This photograph shows the top, or summit, of Mount Everest. Strong winds are blowing snow off the top.

Rainy seasons

India has two main seasons. One is very rainy, and the other is very dry. These changing seasons are caused by the way the wind blows, and are called monsoons. The monsoons affect when crops can grow.

Great Wall of China

The people of China built an amazing wall hundreds of years ago, to protect their country from enemies. The Great Wall of China passes through deserts, mountains and grasslands along the northern edge of China. It is so long, it can be seen from space.

In winter, monsoon winds blow from the land out to sea. This is the dry season.

In summer, monsoon winds blow in from the sea, bringing rain. This is the wet season.

Internet link

For a link to a website where you can take a quiz and reach the top of Mount Everest, go to **www.usborne-quicklinks.com**

The Great Wall of China is made of stone. These watch-towers helped soldiers see their enemies coming.

Many ways of life

Some areas of Asia have hardly any people living in them, but others are very crowded. People across Asia have lots of different beliefs and customs. Ancient traditions often survive alongside modern ways of life.

Tallest buildings

The tallest buildings in the world are the Petronas Towers in Kuala Lumpur, the capital city of Malaysia. They are 452m (1,438ft) high, and have 88 floors, which are used for offices.

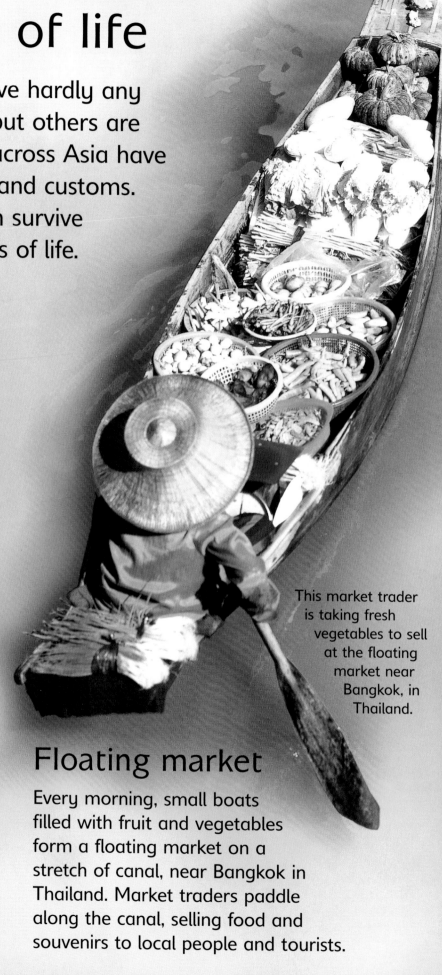

This market trader is taking fresh vegetables to sell at the floating market near Bangkok, in Thailand.

The Petronas Towers are much taller than other skyscrapers nearby.

Floating market

Every morning, small boats filled with fruit and vegetables form a floating market on a stretch of canal, near Bangkok in Thailand. Market traders paddle along the canal, selling food and souvenirs to local people and tourists.

Crowded country

China has the biggest population of any country. Over one-fifth of all the people in the world live there. Most of them live in big cities, though. In some parts of China, there are no people at all.

This map shows where most people live in China.

Internet link

For a link to a website where you can see slide shows and read about Asian countries, go to **www.usborne-quicklinks.com**

Key
people in each km²
(0.39 sq miles)

- None (deserts)
- Fewer than 1
- Up to 100
- More than 100

Glittering spires

Many of the world's religions started in Asia. Buddhism began in India and spread to other Asian countries, including Burma. There are many Buddhist temples in Burma. They are often decorated with pointed spires and large gold statues.

These golden spires are part of a Buddhist temple in Mandalay, Burma.

ATLANTIC

OCEAN

Mediterranean Se

Oran
Algiers
Tunis
TUNISIA
Tripoli
Benghaz
Casablanca
Rabat
MOROCCO
Marrakech
Atlas Mountains
ALGERIA
LIBYA
Laayoune
SAHARA DESER
Ahaggar Mountains
Tibesti Mountains

Tropic of Cancer

WESTERN SAHARA
(Morocco)

MAURITANIA
Nouakchott
MALI
Tombouctou (Timbuktu)
_Sa h e l_
NIGER
CHAD
Lake Chad
Ndjamena

CAPE VERDE
Praia
Senegal
Dakar
SENEGAL
Banjul
THE GAMBIA
Bissau
GUINEA-BISSAU
Niger
Bamako
GUINEA
Niamey
Ouagadougou
BURKINA FASO
BENIN
Kano
NIGERIA
Freetown
Conakry
SIERRA LEONE
IVORY COAST
TOGO
Lake Volta
GHANA
Niger
Abuja

Monrovia
LIBERIA
Yamoussoukro
Accra
Lome
Porto-Novo
Lagos
CAMEROON
Yaounde
CENT AFRI REPU
Bangui
Malabo
EQUATORIAL GUINEA

Equator

SAO TOME AND PRINCIPE
Libreville
GABON
CONGO
Brazzaville
Kinshasa

ATLANTIC

OCEAN

Luanda
Benguela
ANGOLA

Africa

Africa is the second largest continent, and the hottest. It stretches from the Mediterranean Sea in the north, across the equator, and far into the southern hemisphere.

Namib Desert
NAMIBIA
Walvis Bay
Windh
Tropic of Capricorn
Kal De

Internet link

For a link to a website where you can find out all about daily life in five African countries, go to **www.usborne-quicklinks.com**

Key to Africa map

- ■ Capital city
- ○ Major city or town
- ━ Border (where one country joins another one)
- ─ River
- ▬ Coast

Scale

| 0km | 1,000km |
| 0 miles | 620 miles |

Cape Town
Cape of Good Hope
Orang

The sandy brown areas on this satellite picture show how much of Africa is desert. The Sahara Desert is at the top of the continent.

Map labels

Alexandria
Cairo Suez
EGYPT
Nile
Aswan
Tropic of Cancer
Lake Nasser
...awf
...an ...ert

Port Sudan
Red Sea
ERITREA
Asmara
Khartoum
SUDAN
Blue Nile
El Obeid
White Nile
Lake Tana
DJIBOUTI Djibouti
Ethiopian
Highlands
Addis Ababa
ETHIOPIA
SOMALIA
Juba
UGANDA
Lake Turkana
Mogadishu
Equator
Kisangani
Kampala
KENYA
Lake Victoria
Kigali RWANDA
Nairobi
ONGO
Bujumbura
MOCRATIC
BURUNDI
Mwanza
Kilimanjaro
Mombasa
Victoria
PUBLIC)
Lake Tanganyika
Dodoma
SEYCHELLES
TANZANIA
Dar es Salaam
INDIAN
Lubumbashi
COMOROS
Moroni
OCEAN
Ndola
Lake Nyasa (Lake Malawi)
ZAMBIA
Lilongwe
Lusaka Zambezi
MALAWI
Lake Kariba
Nampula
Harare
MOZAMBIQUE
Toamasina
ZIMBABWE
Antananarivo
MAURITIUS
Bulawayo
Beira
Mozambique Channel
MADAGASCAR
Port Louis
SWANA
...rone
Tropic of Capricorn
Pretoria Maputo
...nesburg
Mbabane
Lobamba SWAZILAND
...mfontein Maseru
...UTH LESOTHO
...RICA
Durban
...rakensberg
Port Elizabeth

Africa facts

Total land area *30,311,690km²*
(11,703,343 sq miles)

Biggest country Sudan *2,505,810km²*
(967,493 sq miles)

Smallest country Seychelles *455km²*
(176 sq miles)

Biggest island Madagascar *587,040km²*
(226,660 sq miles)

Highest mountain Kilimanjaro, Tanzania
5,895m (19,340ft)

Longest river River Nile, from Burundi to
Egypt *6,671km (4,145 miles)*

Biggest lake Lake Victoria, Tanzania
69,215km² (26,724 miles)

Highest waterfall Tugela Falls, South
Africa *610m (2,000ft)*

Biggest desert Sahara
9,100,000km²
(3,500,000 sq miles)

This lion's sandy brown coat helps it blend in with its surroundings in its dry African grassland home.

Vast desert

A large part of Africa is covered by the Sahara, the biggest desert in the world. It's very hot there during the day, but at night the temperature often drops below freezing.

Dry desert

Hardly any rain falls in the Sahara Desert. The driest part is in Libya, where the desert is sandy. The wind blows the sand into huge piles called dunes, that form dramatic, curving shapes.

This map shows the different kinds of landscapes in Africa.

Sahara Desert

Key

- Highlands
- Scrub
- Desert
- Rainforest

Savannah grasslands

Internet link

For a link to a website where you can discover more about the wildlife and people who live in the Sahara Desert, go to **www.usborne-quicklinks.com**

One of the best ways to cross the Sahara Desert is by camel. Camels can go a long time without water.

34

Thick rainforest

Some places in Africa have plenty of rain. The island of Madagascar is covered in thick, green rainforest. Many unusual animals, such as small, furry lemurs, live there.

Grassy plains

Large parts of Africa are hot grasslands called savannah. It's too dry there for many trees to grow, but there is enough rain for grasses. Savannah animals include lions, giraffes, elephants and zebras.

Ring-tailed lemurs live in the rainforests of Madagascar.

These zebras live in the savannah grasslands. The distant mountain is Kilimanjaro.

Farms and cities

Many people in Africa live in villages and work on farms. But now more and more people are moving to big cities to work and live.

This map shows the farming areas of Africa.

This is the Sahara Desert. No crops can grow here.

Thick rainforest

Key

● Farmland for crops and animals

○ Land not used for farming

This Zulu woman is carrying water in a clay pot.

Not enough water

Many parts of Africa don't get much rain. When there is too little rain, crops can't grow and people don't have enough water. This is called a drought. Sometimes, water may be carried or brought in pipes to a village where there is a drought.

Internet link

For a link to a website where you can find pictures and stories about life in Africa, as well as some fun things to do, go to **www.usborne-quicklinks.com**

Farming for money

There are farms in most parts of Africa. Some grow grains such as corn or millet for people living nearby to eat. Others grow crops such as coffee or cocoa, to sell to other countries.

Selling crops is a good way for a country to make money. But it may mean that the people can't grow enough food to eat themselves.

This man is picking tea in Burundi. The dried leaves will be sold to countries far away.

Growing city

Cape Town is one of the three capital cities of South Africa. It is built on flat land, close to the Pacific Ocean, around the base of Table Mountain. Cape Town is a growing city. More and more people are moving there from the countryside to find better places to live and work.

This is Cape Town, in South Africa. The nearby mountain is covered in cloud.

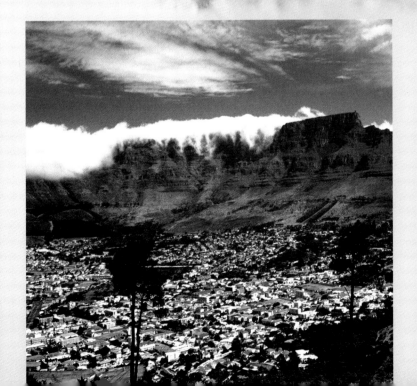

Europe

Europe is a small continent, but it has many countries in it. Only the part of Russia west of the Ural Mountains is in Europe – the rest is in Asia.

Europe is home to many types of birds, such as this common European kingfisher.

Arctic Circle

ARCTIC OCEAN

■ Reykjavik
ICELAND

Norwegian Sea

SWEDEN

British Isles

NORWAY
○ Bergen
Oslo ■

Stockholm
Lake Vanern

○ Edinburgh

○ Belfast

North Sea

DENMARK
Copenhagen ■

Baltic

○ Gothenburg

IRELAND
○ Dublin

UNITED KINGDOM

Gda...

POLA...

○ Cardiff
● **London**

○ Hamburg

Amsterdam
NETHERLANDS
The Hague

Berlin ■

ATLANTIC

English Channel

Brussels
BELGIUM

Rhine

GERMANY

Elbe

Od...

OCEAN

Seine

LUXEMBOURG
Luxembourg ■

Prague

CZECH REPUBLIC

● **Paris**

○ Nantes

Loire

Danube

○ Munich

Vienna ■
Austria

Bratis...

FRANCE

Bern ■
SWITZERLAND

LIECHTENSTEIN
Vaduz

Budap...

Bay of Biscay

○ Lyon

The Alps

○ Milan

Po

SLOVENIA
Ljubljana

Zagreb

CROATIA

○ Bordeaux

○ Turin

Adriatic Sea

BOSNIA AN... HERZEGOVI...

○ Bilbao

Andorra la Vella

MONACO

SAN MARINO

Sarajevo

○ Oporto

ANDORRA

○ Marseille

Corsica (France)

ITALY

AL...

PORTUGAL

Madrid ■

○ Barcelona

Rome ■ **VATICAN CITY**

Ti...

Lisbon ■

Tagus

SPAIN

○ Valencia

Sardinia (Italy)

○ Naples

○ Cordoba

○ Gibraltar (U.K.)

Mediterranean Sea

Sicily (Italy)

MALTA ■ **Valletta**

Key to Europe map

- ■ Capital city
- ○ Major city or town
- ▬ Border (where one country joins another one)
- ― River
- ▬ Coast

Scale

0km   500km
0 miles   310 miles

North Cape

Barents Sea

Murmansk

*Kola
Peninsula*

pland

Oulu

FINLAND

Arkhangelsk

Pechora

Ukhta

Arctic Circle

The rest
of Russia
is in Asia.

Ural Mountains

Northern Dvina

Lake Onega

R U S S I A

Perm

sinki

St. Petersburg

Cherepovets

Tallinn

ESTONIA

Lake Ladoga

*Rybinsk
Reservoir*

Volga

Kama

Kazan

Nizhniy Novgorod

Riga

LATVIA

Moscow

Samara

THUANIA

Vilnius

A

Tula

Don

Volga

Minsk

saw

BELARUS

istula

Voronezh

w

Kiev

Kharkiv

Volgograd

Dnieper

Lviv

UKRAINE

Donetsk

Don

Volga

Astrakhan

Dnipropetrovsk

VAKIA

Carpathian Mountains

MOLDOVA

Rostov

*Caspian
Sea*

GARY

Cluj-Napoca

Chisinau

Odesa

*Sea of
Azov*

*Crimean
Peninsula*

ROMANIA

grade

Bucharest

Danube

Caucasus Mountains

Mount Elbrus

Black Sea

A AND

ENEGRO

BULGARIA

Sofia

Skopje

ACEDONIA

EECE

*Aegean
Sea*

Athens

*Crete
(Greece)*

This satellite photograph
shows how Europe joins
onto Asia. The big, white
patch at the top is the ice
that covers the Arctic.

Europe facts

Total land area 10,205,720km²
(3,940,428 sq miles)

Biggest country Russia
*Total area: 17,075,200km²
(6,492,735 sq miles)
Area of European Russia:
4,294,400km² (658,068 sq miles)*

Smallest country Vatican City
0.44km² *(0.17 sq miles)*

Biggest island Great Britain
229,870km² *(90,506 sq miles)*

Highest mountain Mount Elbrus,
Russia 5,642m *(18,510ft)*

Longest river Volga 3,700km
(2,298 miles)

Biggest lake Lake Ladoga, Russia
17,700km² *(6,834 sq miles)*

Highest waterfall Utigard, on
the Jostedal Glacier, Norway
800m *(2,625ft)*

Biggest desert There are no
deserts in Europe.

Internet link

For a link to a website where you
can explore a virtual castle, like one
you might find in Europe, go to
www.usborne-quicklinks.com

Farms and hills

A lot of the land in Europe is gently hilly and good for farming. Some areas are rocky or snowy, and fewer crops grow there.

This map shows some of the crops that grow in Europe.

Key

- Grapes
- Olives (for oil)
- Fruit
- Potatoes
- Grains, such as wheat and barley

Europe

Asia

Mediterranean Sea

Fruit and vegetables

The south of Europe is on the coast of the Mediterranean Sea. The weather there is very hot and dry in summer, but cool and wet in winter. Oranges, lemons and other citrus fruits grow well there, as well as many other kinds of fruit and vegetables.

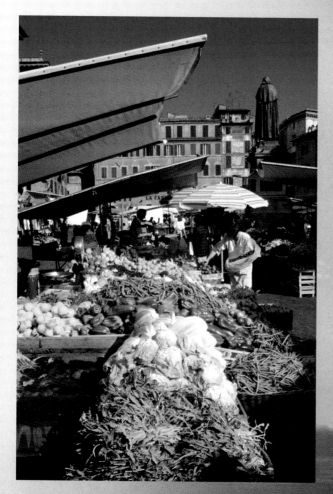

This market is in Rome, in Italy. Every day, people bring fresh fruit and vegetables from the farms nearby, to sell at the market.

Natural hot water

The island of Iceland has natural hot water, heated by rocks under the Earth. From time to time, jets of steam and hot water burst out through holes in the ground. These jets are called geysers.

This is Strokkur Geyser, in Iceland. Boiling hot water erupts from it every few minutes.

Jagged peaks

The largest group of mountains in Europe is the Alps. They formed millions of years ago, out of giant folds of rock. They have very jagged shapes, which were carved out by rivers of ice, called glaciers.

This picture shows how some of the valleys and lower slopes of the Alps are used for farming crops. Behind, you can see much higher, snowy peaks.

Internet link

For a link to a website where you can visit European countries and see slide shows, go to **www.usborne-quicklinks.com**

Places to see

Europe is famous for its beautiful old cities and historic buildings. But many exciting modern buildings attract visitors too.

Eiffel Tower

The Eiffel Tower was built in 1889, in Paris, the capital city of France. Until 1930, it was the tallest tower in the world. Since it was built, more than 200 million people have visited it.

The Eiffel Tower in France is as tall as over 100 trucks stacked on top of each other.

Great cathedrals

Many cities in Europe have huge churches called cathedrals. They are made of carved stone, and took many years to build. Some have pointed spires on top, others have towers or rounded domes.

This is Cologne Cathedral in Germany. It took 600 years to build.

Modern buildings

There are some amazing modern buildings in Europe. One of the most interesting is Spain's Museo Guggenheim Bilbao. It is covered with huge curving sheets of metal.

This is the Museo Guggenheim Bilbao in Spain. It is a gallery where people go to look at modern art.

Roman remains

About 2,000 years ago, Rome was one of the biggest cities in the world. At that time, the Romans ruled all the lands around the Mediterranean Sea. Ruins of Roman buildings can still be seen in lots of places in Europe.

Internet link

For a link to a website where you can find out more about the Eiffel Tower and crazy tower stunts, go to **www.usborne-quicklinks.com**

This map shows where the Romans ruled in Europe. These lands were called the Roman Empire.

Europe

Rome

Asia

These are the remains of the Colosseum in Rome. People came here to see fighters called gladiators.

Key

⬤ The Roman Empire

Oceania

Oceania is the smallest continent. It is made up of Australia, New Zealand and Papua New Guinea, as well as many smaller islands dotted across the Pacific Ocean.

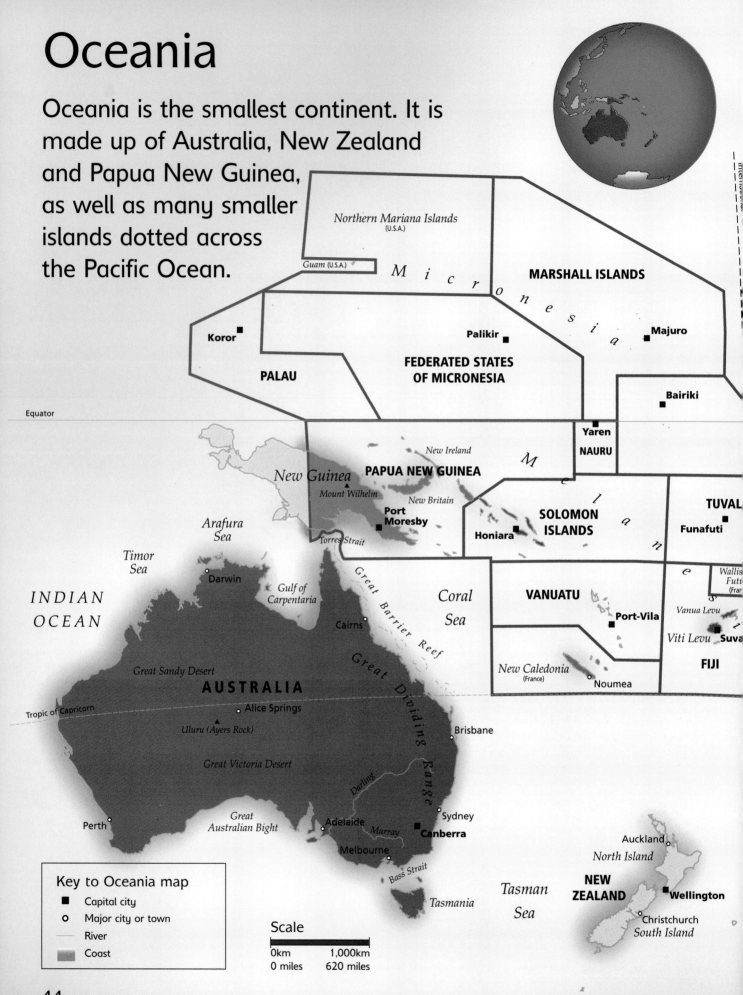

Northern Mariana Islands (U.S.A.)

Guam (U.S.A.)

M i c r o n e s i a

MARSHALL ISLANDS

Koror ■

Palikir ■

Majuro ■

PALAU

FEDERATED STATES OF MICRONESIA

Bairiki ■

Equator

Yaren ■
NAURU

New Ireland

PAPUA NEW GUINEA

M e l a n

New Guinea

▲ *Mount Wilhelm*

New Britain

Port Moresby

SOLOMON ISLANDS

e s i a

TUVAL

Funafuti ■

Arafura Sea

Torres Strait

Honiara ■

Wallis Futt (Fran

Timor Sea

Darwin ○

Gulf of Carpentaria

Coral Sea

VANUATU

Vanua Levu

INDIAN OCEAN

Cairns ○

Great Barrier Reef

Port-Vila ■

Viti Levu **Suva**

Great Sandy Desert

AUSTRALIA

Great Dividing Range

New Caledonia (France)

Noumea ○

FIJI

Tropic of Capricorn

○ Alice Springs

▲ *Uluru (Ayers Rock)*

Great Victoria Desert

Darling

Brisbane ○

Perth ○

Great Australian Bight

Adelaide ○

Murray

Sydney ○

Canberra ■

Melbourne ○

Bass Strait

Tasman Sea

Auckland ○

North Island

NEW ZEALAND

Wellington ■

Tasmania

Christchurch ○
South Island

Key to Oceania map

- ■ Capital city
- ○ Major city or town
- — River
-   Coast

Scale

| 0km | 1,000km |
| 0 miles | 620 miles |

Oceania facts

Total land area 8,564,400km² (3,306,715 sq miles)

Biggest country Australia 7,741,220km² (2,988,885 sq miles)

Smallest country Nauru 21km² (8 sq miles)

Biggest island New Guinea 800,000km² (309,000 sq miles)

Highest mountain Mount Wilhelm, Papua New Guinea 4,509m (14,793ft)

Longest river Murray/Darling River Australia 3,718km (2,310 miles)

Biggest lake Lake Eyre, Australia 9,000km² (3,470 sq miles)

Highest waterfall Sutherland Falls on the Arthur River, New Zealand 580m (1,904ft)

Biggest desert Great Victoria Desert, Australia 388,500km² (150,000 sq miles)

P o l y n e s i a

Equator

PACIFIC OCEAN

KIRIBATI

Tokelau (New Zealand)

AMOA
Apia

American Samoa (U.S.A.)

Cook Islands (New Zealand)

IGA
alofa

Niue (New Zealand)

Tahiti

French Polynesia (France)

Tropic of Capricorn

Pitcairn Islands (U.K.)

International Date Line

Some of the countries in Oceania are made up of hundreds of islands, which are too small to be seen on this map. The red lines show where one country ends and another begins.

This photograph was taken from space. The light brown areas show that much of Australia is desert. The large, white area below Australia is Antarctica.

Internet links

For a link to a website where you can take a trip to Australia and see a slide show, go to **www.usborne-quicklinks.com**

Wallabies live in the dry, dusty grasslands of Australia. Their long eyelashes protect their eyes from blowing sand.

Desert and ocean

Oceania is made up of over 20,000 islands in the Pacific Ocean. Most of them are tiny, but the desert land of Australia is huge. Many small islands are the tops of underwater volcanoes.

The deepest place

The bottom of the Pacific Ocean is covered in mountains, and valleys called trenches. The deepest place on Earth is in the Mariana Trench. It is over 11km (6.8 miles) deep. If you dropped a small rock into the sea, it would take over an hour to reach the bottom of the Mariana Trench.

These maps show the Mariana Trench and the Challenger Deep, which is its deepest part.

Japan (Asia)

Philippines (Asia)

Mariana Islands

Mariana Islands (enlarged)

Guam

Key

Islands

Trench

Challenger Deep

Ancient land

Most of Australia is a bare, rocky desert. Its land has hardly changed for millions of years. The rocks have slowly been worn into smooth shapes by the wind and rain.

Wave Rock in Australia looks like a towering wall of water. It was worn into this unusual shape by the wind and rain.

Internet link

For a link to a website where you can explore a coral reef and its creatures, go to **www.usborne-quicklinks.com**

How islands form

The oldest islands in Oceania are made of limestone rock. The youngest islands are the tips of underwater volcanoes. These pictures show how an island forms and changes.

A volcano grows under the sea and rises up above the surface. When it stops erupting, animals and plants live on it.

Sea animals called corals grow around the edge of the dead volcano. They form a ring of coral called an atoll.

The coral dies and forms hard limestone. Forests grow on these new islands. The soft rock of the volcano is slowly worn away by the sea.

The middle part of this island in French Polynesia is a volcano. It is surrounded by coral reefs, which are large areas of tiny sea animals called corals.

Forests by the sea

Mangrove trees live on the edge of warm seas, with their roots partly underwater. Unlike most plants, they aren't harmed by salty sea water. Thick mangrove forests grow in Papua New Guinea and other islands in Oceania.

The roots of mangrove trees spread out wide and prop the trees up in the swampy ground.

Ocean living

Fewer people live in Oceania than on any other continent apart from Antarctica. Most of Oceania's people live near the sea.

Most Australians live near the sea, and many enjoy water sports. This man has found a good wave to surf, near a beach in Australia.

Australia's people

Four out of five Australians live in towns and cities that are within one hour's drive of the sea. The rest live scattered across the huge desert area called the outback. People there live so far apart that some children have to do their schoolwork by mail or over the Internet.

This map shows how many people live in different parts of Australia.

Key
people in each km² (0.39 sq miles)

● More than 50   2 – 4

● 4–50   1 – 2

Fewer than 1

Original people

Most people in Australia and New Zealand today are related to people who came from Europe. But the first people in Australia were the Aboriginal people, thousands of years before. The first settlers in New Zealand were the Maoris.

These men are wearing traditional Maori costumes. All children in New Zealand learn about Maori traditions at school.

Internet link

For a link to a website with a selection of photographs from Papua New Guinea, go to **www.usborne-quicklinks.com**

Fiji's farmers

Many Fijians are farmers. They grow enough food, such as corn and vegetables, for their families and other people in their villages. Some of their crops, such as coconuts and sugar cane, are sold to other countries.

Farming people on Fiji often live in one-room houses like these, with thatched roofs and woven floor mats inside.

Dressing up

The Huli people live in the mountains of Papua New Guinea. Huli men paint their faces and dress in spectacular feathered wigs to perform dances, which are famous all over the world.

This Huli man is putting on face paint. His wig is made from grasses, and feathers from a bird called a cassowary.

The Arctic

The area around the North Pole is called the Arctic. There's no land at the North Pole, but the sea there is so cold that its surface freezes and turns to thick ice.

The white patch on this globe shows the parts of the Arctic that are always covered with ice.

Frozen land

The Arctic Circle is an imaginary line around the Arctic. Eight countries have land inside the Arctic Circle. This land is called tundra. The soil there is frozen for most of the year. No trees can grow, but lichen and moss plants grow close to the ground.

Internet link

For a link to a website where you can take part in a quiz about animals that live in the Arctic, go to **www.usborne-quicklinks.com**

Coping with cold

Arctic animals have to survive freezing temperatures. Many have thick, bushy white coats to keep them warm and help them blend in with the snow. Some have a layer of fat for extra warmth.

This baby harp seal has thick fur, and a layer of fat under its skin to keep it warm.

Scale

0km   1,000km
0 miles   620 miles

PACIFIC

OCEAN

Aleutian Islands

Bering Sea

○Anchorage

ALASKA (U.S.A.)

Arctic Circle

○Anadyr

JAPAN
Sapporo

○Petropavlosk-Kamchatskiy

RUSSIA

Rocky Mountains

Yukon

Chukchi Sea

Wrangel Island

East Siberian Sea

Verkhoyansk Range

Lena

Beaufort Sea

New Siberia Islands

Laptev Sea

○Yellowknife

Victoria Island

Queen Elizabeth Islands

North Magnetic Pole

Severnaya Zemlya

A R C T I C

+ North Pole

O C E A N

Yenisey

CANADA

Ellesmere Island

Franz Josef Land

Kara Sea

Baffin Island

Novaya Zemlya

Ob

Baffin Bay

Svalbard (Norway)

Ural Mountains

Yekaterinburg○

GREENLAND (Denmark)

Barents Sea

RUSSIA

Davis Strait

Greenland Sea

○Murmansk

■ **Godthab**

Arkhangelsk○

Norwegian Sea

Arctic Circle

FINLAND

Nizhniy Novgorod○

■ **Reykjavik**

ICELAND

SWEDEN

Helsinki ■

■ **Moscow**

Faroe Islands (Denmark)

ESTONIA

NORWAY

LATVIA

ATLANTIC

Oslo ■   **Stockholm** ■

Baltic Sea

LITHUANIA

OCEAN

North Sea

RUSSIA

BELARUS

DENMARK

IRELAND

UNITED KINGDOM

GERMANY

POLAND

UKRAINE

NETHERLANDS

MOLDOVA

BELGIUM

CZECH REPUBLIC

SLOVAKIA

ROMANIA

Key to Arctic map

■ Capital city

○ Major city or town

▬ Border (where one country joins another one)

— River

▓ Coast

The Antarctic

The Antarctic, also called Antarctica, is the continent at the South Pole. It is the coldest and windiest continent. The land is covered with ice over 2,000m (6,500ft) thick. Nine-tenths of all the world's ice is in the Antarctic.

The Antarctic is at the bottom of the Earth. It is surrounded by the Southern Ocean.

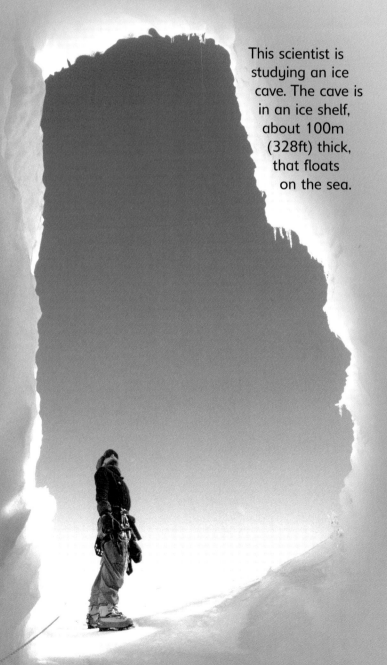

This scientist is studying an ice cave. The cave is in an ice shelf, about 100m (328ft) thick, that floats on the sea.

Home for scientists

People started exploring the Antarctic just over 100 years ago. The only people who live there today are scientists. They study the weather, ice and rocks to try to find out more about life on Earth.

Keeping warm

The Antarctic is home to thousands of penguins. They have layers of fat underneath their feathers to protect them from the cold, and huddle together in big groups for extra warmth. Penguins take turns standing at the edge of the group, where it's windy and much colder.

Internet link

For a link to a website featuring Antarctic maps, satellite views, animals and even jokes go to **www.usborne-quicklinks.com**

South Sandwich
Islands
(U.K.)

South Georgia
(U.K.)

Antarctic Circle

South Orkney Islands
(U.K.)

South Shetland Islands
(U.K.)

Queen Maud Land

*Weddell
Sea*

*Coats
Land*

*Enderby
Land*

*Antarctic
Peninsula*

ANTARCTICA

*East
Antarctica*

*Ronne
Ice Shelf*

*Bellingshausen
Sea*

▲
Vinson Massif
5,140m
(16,863ft)

*Ellsworth
Land*

+ South Pole

*West
Antarctica*

Transantarctic Mountains

*Amundsen
Sea*

Marie Byrd Land

*Ross
Ice Shelf*

Wilkes Land

Ross Sea

*Victoria
Land*

South Magnetic
Pole +

Antarctic Circle

Scale

0km	1,000km
0 miles	620 miles

*SOUTHERN
OCEAN*

Key to Antarctic map

▲ Mountain

▬ Coast

This emperor penguin chick is
keeping warm by standing on
its mother's feet and snuggling
up against her tummy.

Flags of the world

North America

Antigua and Barbuda

Bahamas

Barbados

Belize

Canada

Costa Rica

Cuba

Dominica

Dominican Republic

El Salvador

Grenada

Guatemala

Haiti

Honduras

Jamaica

Mexico

Nicaragua

Panama

St. Kitts and Nevis

St. Lucia

St. Vincent and the Grenadines

Trinidad and Tobago

United States of America

South America

Argentina

Bolivia

Brazil

Chile

Colombia

Ecuador

Guyana

Paraguay

Peru

Surinam

Uruguay

Venezuela

Asia

Afghanistan

Armenia

Azerbaijan

Bahrain

Bangladesh

Bhutan

Brunei

Burma (Myanmar)

Cambodia

China

East Timor

Georgia

Asia (continued)

 India

 Indonesia

 Iran

 Iraq

 Israel

 Japan

 Jordan

 Kazakhstan

 Kuwait

 Kyrgyzstan

 Laos

 Lebanon

 Malaysia

 Maldives

 Mongolia

 Nepal

 North Korea

 Oman

 Pakistan

 Philippines

 Qatar

 Russian Federation

 Saudi Arabia

 Singapore

 South Korea

 Sri Lanka

 Syria

 Taiwan

 Tajikistan

Thailand

 Turkey

 Turkmenistan

 United Arab Emirates

 Uzbekistan

 Vietnam

 Yemen

Africa

 Algeria

 Angola

 Benin

 Botswana

Burkina Faso

 Burundi

 Cameroon

 Cape Verde

 Central African Republic

 Chad

Comoros

Congo

 Congo
(Democratic Republic)

 Djibouti

Egypt

 Equatorial Guinea

Eritrea

 Ethiopia

Africa (continued)

Gabon

The Gambia

Ghana

Guinea

Guinea-Bissau

Ivory Coast

Kenya

Lesotho

Liberia

Libya

Madagascar

Malawi

Mali

Mauritania

Mauritius

Morocco

Mozambique

Namibia

Niger

Nigeria

Rwanda

Sao Tome and
Principe

Senegal

Seychelles

Sierra Leone

Somalia

South Africa

Sudan

Swaziland

Tanzania

Togo

Tunisia

Uganda

Zambia

Zimbabwe

Europe

Albania

Andorra

Austria

Belarus

Belgium

Bosnia and
Herzegovina

Bulgaria

Croatia

Cyprus

Czech Republic

Denmark

Estonia

Finland

France

Germany

Greece

Hungary

Iceland

Europe (continued)

 Ireland

 Italy

 Latvia

 Liechtenstein

 Lithuania

 Luxembourg

 Macedonia

 Malta

 Moldova

 Monaco

 Netherlands

 Norway

 Poland

 Portugal

 Romania

 Russian Federation

 San Marino

 Serbia and Montenegro

 Slovakia

 Slovenia

 Spain

 Sweden

 Switzerland

 Turkey

 Ukraine

 United Kingdom

 Vatican City

Oceania

 Australia

 Federated States of Micronesia

 Fiji

 Kiribati

Marshall Islands

Nauru

New Zealand

Palau

Papau New Guinea

Samoa

Solomon Islands

Tonga

Tuvalu

Vanuatu

Changing flags

Flags of the world change frequently. New flags are invented as new countries are born, or their situation changes.

For example, in 1991, there were important changes to the way South Africa was run. All adults in the country were allowed to vote in free elections for the first time. To celebrate this, a new flag was designed.

New flag of South Africa

South African flag until 1994

Internet links

For a link to a website with flags and facts, go to **www.usborne-quicklinks.com**

Map index

This is an index of all the places and features named on the maps. Each entry may contain the following parts: the name of the country, place or feature (in **bold** type), the country or region where a place or feature is (in *italic* type), and the page(s) where it can be found (in plain type). Some names also have a description explaining exactly what kind of place they are, for example, capital cities or rivers.

A

Abu Dhabi *United Arab Emirates, capital* 26
Abuja *Nigeria, capital* 32
Acapulco *Mexico* 14
Accra *Ghana, capital* 32
Aconcagua *Argentina, mountain* 10, 20
Addis Ababa *Ethiopia, capital* 33
Adelaide *Australia* 44
Aden *Yemen* 26
Adriatic Sea *Europe* 38
Aegean Sea *Europe* 39
Afghanistan 13, 26
Africa 11, 32–33, 34, 36
Ahaggar Mountains *Africa, mountain range* 32
Al Jawf *Libya* 33
Alaska *United States of America* 10, 12, 14, 51
Alaska, Gulf of *North America* 10, 14
Albania 13, 38
Aleutian Islands *United States of America, islands* 10, 51
Alexandria *Egypt* 33
Algeria 12, 32
Algiers *Algeria, capital* 32
Alice Springs *Australia* 44
Almaty *Kazakhstan* 26
Alps, the *Europe, mountain range* 38
Altai Mountains *Asia, mountain range* 11, 20, 26
Amazon *South America, river* 6, 10, 20, 21
Amazon Rainforest *South America* 6, 10, 20
American Samoa *Oceania, islands* 45
Amman *Jordan, capital* 26
Amsterdam *Netherlands, capital* 38
Amundsen Sea *Antarctica* 53
Amur *Asia, river* 11, 27
Anadyr *Russia* 27, 51
Anchorage *Alaska* 14, 51
Andes *South America, mountain range* 6, 10, 20
Andorra 8, 38
Andorra la Vella *Andorra, capital* 8, 38
Angola 13, 32
Ankara *Turkey, capital* 26

Antananarivo *Madagascar, capital* 33
Antarctic Peninsula *Antarctica* 10, 53
Antarctica 11, 13, 53
Antigua and Barbuda 15
Apia *Samoa, capital* 45
Appalachian Mountains *United States of America, mountain range* 10, 15
Aqtobe *Kazakhstan* 26
Arabia *Asia* 11
Arabian Sea *Indian Ocean* 11, 26
Arafura Sea *Asia/Oceania* 11, 27, 44
Aral Sea *Asia* 11, 26
Arctic Ocean 11, 13, 14, 26, 38, 51
Argentina 12, 20–21
Arkansas *United States of America, river* 15
Arkhangelsk *Russia* 26, 39, 51
Armenia 13, 26
Ashgabat *Turkmenistan, capital* 26
Asia 11, 26–27
Asmara *Eritrea, capital* 33
Astana *Kazakhstan, capital* 26
Astrakhan *Russia* 26, 39
Asuncion *Paraguay, capital* 21
Aswan *Egypt* 33
Atacama Desert *South America* 6, 10, 20
Athabasca, Lake *Canada* 14
Athens *Greece, capital* 39
Atlanta *United States of America* 15
Atlantic Ocean 10, 12, 15, 21, 32, 38, 51
Atlas Mountains *Africa, mountain range* 10, 32
Auckland *New Zealand* 44
Australia 13, 44, 48
Austria 13, 38
Azerbaijan 13, 26
Azores *Atlantic Ocean, islands* 10, 12
Azov, Sea of *Europe* 39

B

Baffin Bay *Canada* 10, 15, 51
Baffin Island *Canada, island* 10, 15, 51
Baghdad *Iraq, capital* 26

Bahamas, the 12, 15
Bahrain 13, 26
Baikal, Lake *Russia* 11, 27
Bairiki *Kiribati, capital* 44
Baku *Azerbaijan, capital* 26
Balbina Reservoir *Brazil* 20–21
Balkhash, Lake *Kazakhstan* 26
Baltic Sea *Europe* 38, 51
Bamako *Mali, capital* 32
Banda Sea *Indonesia* 27
Bangalore *India* 26
Bangkok *Thailand, capital* 27
Bangladesh 13, 26
Bangui *Central African Republic, capital* 32
Banjul *the Gambia, capital* 32
Baotou *China* 27
Barbados 15
Barcelona *Spain* 38
Barents Sea *Europe* 11, 26, 39, 51
Basra *Iraq* 26
Bass Strait *Australia* 44
Beaufort Sea *North America* 10, 14, 51
Beijing *China, capital* 27
Beira *Mozambique* 33
Beirut *Lebanon, capital* 26
Belarus 13, 39, 51
Belem *Brazil* 21
Belfast *United Kingdom* 38
Belgium 12, 38, 51
Belgrade *Serbia and Montenegro, capital* 39
Belize 12, 15
Bellingshausen Sea *Antarctica* 53
Belmopan *Belize, capital* 15
Belo Horizonte *Brazil* 21
Bengal, Bay of *Asia* 11, 26
Benghazi *Libya* 32
Benguela *Angola* 32
Benin 12, 32
Bergen *Norway* 38
Bering Sea *North America* 11, 14, 27, 51
Bering Strait *United States of America* 14
Berlin *Germany, capital* 38
Bern *Switzerland, capital* 38
Bhutan 13, 26
Bilbao *Spain* 38
Biscay, Bay of *Europe* 8, 38
Bishkek *Kyrgyzstan, capital* 26
Bissau *Guinea-Bissau, capital* 32
Black Sea *Asia/Europe* 11, 13, 26, 39
Bloemfontein *South Africa, capital* 33
Blue Nile *Africa, river* 33
Bogota *Colombia, capital* 20
Bolivia 12, 20
Bordeaux *France* 38
Borneo *Indonesia/Malaysia, island* 11, 27
Bosnia and Herzegovina 13, 38
Boston *United States of America* 15
Botswana 13, 33
Brasilia *Brazil, capital* 21
Bratislava *Slovakia, capital* 38
Brazil 12, 20–21
Brazilian Highlands *Brazil* 21
Brazzaville *Congo, capital* 32
Brisbane *Australia* 44

British Isles *Europe, islands* 10, 38
Brunei 13, 27
Brussels *Belgium, capital* 38
Bucharest *Romania, capital* 39
Budapest *Hungary, capital* 38
Buenos Aires *Argentina, capital* 20
Bujumbura *Burundi, capital* 33
Bulawayo *Zimbabwe* 33
Bulgaria 13, 39
Burkina Faso 12, 32
Burma (**Myanmar**) 13, 27
Burundi 13, 33

C

Cairns *Australia* 44
Cairo *Egypt, capital* 33
Calgary *Canada* 14
Cali *Colombia* 20
California *United States of America* 14
Cambodia 13, 27
Cameroon 13, 32
Canada 7, 12, 14–15, 51
Canary Islands *Atlantic Ocean, islands* 10, 12
Canberra *Australia, capital* 44
Cape Comorin *Asia* 11, 26
Cape Farewell *Greenland* 15
Cape Hatteras *United States of America* 15
Cape Horn *South America* 6, 10, 20
Cape of Good Hope *Africa* 11, 32
Cape Town *South Africa, capital* 32
Cape Verde 10, 12, 32
Caracas *Venezuela, capital* 20
Cardiff *United Kingdom* 38
Caribbean Sea *North America* 6, 10, 12, 15, 20
Carpathian Mountains *Europe, mountain range* 39
Carpentaria, Gulf of *Australia* 44
Casablanca *Morocco* 32
Caspian Sea *Asia* 11, 13, 26, 39
Caucasus Mountains *Asia, mountain range* 26, 39
Cayenne *French Guiana, capital* 21
Celebes *Indonesia, island* 11, 27
Central African Republic 13, 32–33
Central America 6, 10
Chad 13, 32
Chad, Lake *Chad* 32
Chelyabinsk *Russia* 26
Chennai (Madras) *India* 26
Cherepovets *Russia* 39
Chicago *United States of America* 15
Chile 12, 20
China 11, 13, 27, 31
Chisinau *Moldova, capital* 39
Chongqing *China* 27
Christchurch *New Zealand* 44
Chukchi Sea *Arctic Ocean* 51
Cincinnati *United States of America* 15
Ciudad Juarez *Mexico* 14
Cluj-Napoca *Romania* 39
Coats Land *Antarctica* 53

Index

Acknowledgements

Every effort has been made to trace the copyright holders of the material in this book. If any rights have been omitted, the publishers offer to rectify this in any future edition, following notification. The publishers are grateful to the following organizations and individuals for their contribution and permission to reproduce this material.

Cover (Front) Digital Vision, (back) Digital Vision; **1** NASA/Science Photo Library; **2–3** Getty Images/Pal Hermansen; **5** Getty Images/Walter Bibikow; **7** Getty Images/Louise Murray; **8**(b) Dave G. Houser/CORBIS; **14**(bl) Digital Vision; **15**(tr) Julian Baum & David Angus/Science Photo Library; **16**(l) Getty Images/John Giustina; **16–17** Getty Images/Macduff Everton; **17**(tr) Roger Ressmeyer/CORBIS; **18** Powerstock; **19**(tr) Owaki-Kulla/CORBIS, (l) Bryan & Cherry Alexander Photography/Alamy, (br) Getty Images/Doug Armand; **20**(bl) Digital Vision; **21**(tr) Julian Baum & David Angus/Science Photo Library; **22** Galen Rowell/CORBIS; **23**(tl) Powerstock, (r) Owen Franken/CORBIS, (bl) Robert Harding Picture Library Ltd/Alamy; **24** Jim Zuckerman/Alamy; **25**(r) Robert Harding Picture Library Ltd/Alamy, (l) Getty Images/Ary Diesendruck; **26**(bl) Digital Vision; **27**(tr) Julian Baum & David Angus/Science Photo Library; **28**(l) Jon Arnold Images/Alamy, (br) Michael S. Lewis/CORBIS; **29** Miles Ertman/Masterfile; **30**(main) World Pictures, (bl) Macduff Everton/CORBIS; **31**(br) Powerstock; **33**(tr) Tom Van Sant/Geosphere Project, Santa Monica/Science Photo Library, (br) Digital Vision; **34–35**(b) Getty Images/Frans Lemmens; **35**(tr) Getty Images/Nick Garbutt, (m) NHPA/Daryl Balfour; **36** Dallas and John Heaton/Alamy; **37**(tr) Getty Images/Bruno De Hogues, (bl) Getty Images/Stephen Beer; **38**(ml) Digital Vision; **39**(br) Julian Baum & David Angus/Science Photo Library; **40**(bl) Art Kowalsky/Alamy; **40–41**(main) Jon Arnold Images/ Alamy; **41**(mr) Getty Images/Wilfried Krecichwost; **42**(main) Getty Images/John Lawrence, (mr) Getty Images/ Jorg Greuel; **43**(t) Powerstock, (bl) Getty Images/A & L Sinibaldi; **45**(t) Planetary Visions Ltd/Science Photo Library, (b) Digital Vision; **46**(b) Jean Paul Ferrero/Ardea London Ltd; **47**(t) Tim McKenna/CORBIS, (br) Theo Allofs/CORBIS; **48**(t) Mark A. Johnson/CORBIS, (br) Anders Ryman/CORBIS; **49**(ml) Jon Arnold Images/Alamy, (r) Wolfgang Kaehler/CORBIS; **50**(b) W. Perry Conway/CORBIS; **52** Graham Neden, Ecoscene/CORBIS; **53**(br) Tim David/CORBIS.

American editor: Carrie A. Seay